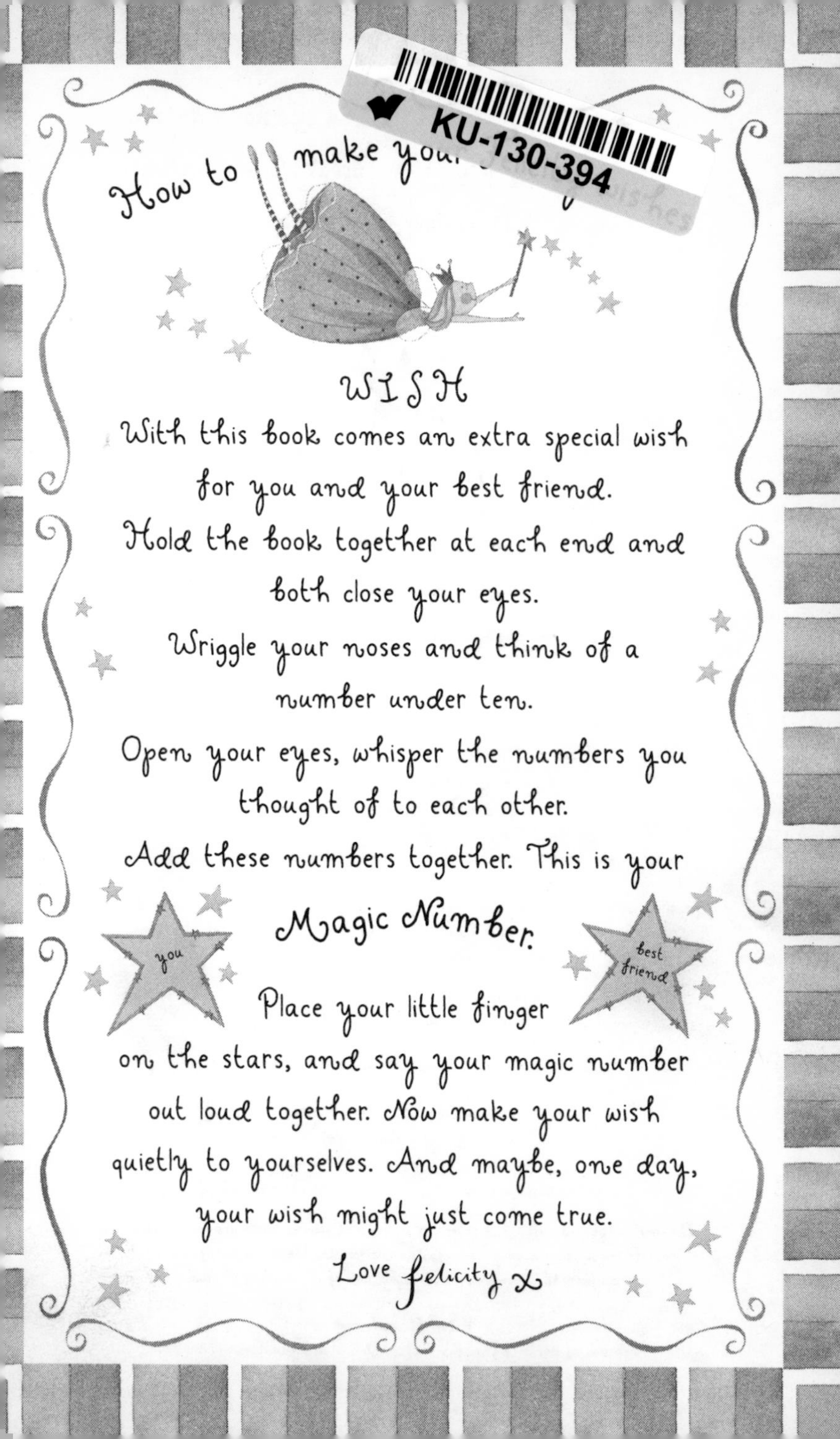

How to make you

WISH

With this book comes an extra special wish for you and your best friend.
Hold the book together at each end and both close your eyes.
Wriggle your noses and think of a number under ten.
Open your eyes, whisper the numbers you thought of to each other.
Add these numbers together. This is your

Magic Number.

Place your little finger on the stars, and say your magic number out loud together. Now make your wish quietly to yourselves. And maybe, one day, your wish might just come true.

Love Felicity x

For Granny Daf' – with thanks for flapjack
and keeping my coffee breaks on schedule!
Much love, Emma x

First published in Great Britain in 2006 by Hodder Children's Books

1

A Catalogue record for this book is available from the British Library

ISBN-10: 0340 911964
ISBN-13: 9780340911969

Printed and bound in Great Britain by Bookmarque Ltd, Croydon, Surrey

The paper and board used in this paperback by Hodder Children's Books are natural recyclable products made from wood grown in sustainable forests. The manufacturing processes conform to the environmental regulations of the country of origin.

Hodder Children's Books
A division of Hachette Children's Books, 338 Euston Road, London NW1 3BH

CONTENTS

Exciting Escapades

Even though Winnie hadn't been at the School of Nine Wishes for long, she no longer felt like a new girl. She had found best friends in Felicity Wishes, Holly, Polly and Daisy, and with them, exciting adventures made new memories each day.

When Felicity and her friends first met Winnie she was shy, quiet and even a little nervous. But one day she went on a life-changing adventure halfway around Fairy World, and she was never quite the same fairy again...

* * *

It was the end of term at the School of Nine Wishes. Although Winnie had made some good friends, Miss Meandering, her form tutor, had noticed that she was still rather shy and sometimes didn't have the confidence to join in with the other fairies. Miss Meandering was sure that there was a more adventurous spirit hiding behind Winnie's shyness.

"Where's Winnie?" asked Felicity, playing leapfrog with Daisy and Polly in the playground at break-time.

"Miss Meandering asked her to stay behind after class," said Polly.

"Oh, I hope she isn't in trouble," said Felicity, landing with a bump.

"You know I'm not one for gossip," said Holly, smiling. "But I've heard a rumour that Miss Meandering is going to ask Winnie to represent the School of Nine Wishes on a visit to our sister school."

"But that doesn't sound like Winnie!" gasped Felicity. "You know she's happiest at home with her close friends."

"Well, almost all gossip starts with something true," said Holly with a wink.

* * *

And the rumour about Winnie was true; only a week later, Felicity and her friends were waving Winnie off on her trip to an island on the other side of Fairy World.

"Promise to write to us," said Felicity, feeling a little teary. She was going to miss her new friend. "I've packed you some chocolate hearts for the journey!"

"And here's a spare pair of tights," said Holly. "Just in case!"

Polly and Daisy gave Winnie presents too. Polly had wrapped up an emergency torch and Daisy gave Winnie a photo of all five of them at Glitter Beach last weekend.

"You're the best friends a fairy could ever have!" called Winnie. "I promise I'll write to you every week!"

The four fairy friends waved frantically as Winnie flew off with a huge bag on her shoulders, a map in one hand and a compass in the other.

Winnie had never been anywhere so far away from home before. Every time she thought of the journey ahead, her tummy would flutter, but she wasn't quite sure whether it was because of nerves or excitement. It was going to be a long journey, but an exciting adventure that she would never forget.

* * *

"Have you heard from Winnie yet?" Polly asked Felicity when the fairy friends met up at Sparkles café the following weekend.

"No, not yet. It's been a week since she left and I don't even know if she has made it to her destination," said Felicity anxiously.

"Don't worry, Felicity. I'm sure she will be fine," said Daisy, trying to reassure herself as much as Felicity.

* * *

A long week later, Felicity heard the

clatter of her letter box and fluttered downstairs as fast as her wings could carry her. There on the mat was what she had been waiting for – a postcard from Winnie!

Dear Felicity, Holly,
Polly and Daisy,

Sorry for not writing before. Our boat sank! Please don't worry. I got everyone off safely. Should reach our sister school very soon and will write more when I can.

Love and wishes,
Winnie xx

To
Felicity Wishes
Little
Blossoming
Near Bloomfield

Felicity looked at the card, perplexed, and then slowly read it again.

* * *

"That's nice," said Holly at school later that day, scanning the postcard and flipping it over to look at the picture of a beach hotel on the front.

Felicity raised her eyebrows.

"Read it again!" she urged Holly. "Would you say that postcard came from a shy, quiet and nervous fairy?"

Daisy peeped over Holly's shoulder at the postcard. "No way!" said Daisy. "You wouldn't get a nervous fairy rescuing everyone from a sinking boat!"

"That's exactly what I thought!" said Felicity.

* * *

Felicity's tiny concerns grew into huge worries when she received Winnie's next postcard, a few days later.

Felicity had begun to suspect that it wasn't Winnie writing the postcards, but someone else! Felicity's teachers were always telling her that she had an overactive imagination, so she fluttered round to see Polly for advice. She knew that Polly was her most sensible friend and could always be relied on to bring her down to earth if necessary.

"You're right!" said Polly, reading between the lines written on the card. "No quiet fairy would ever get up in front of a whole school and give a speech!"

"I knew it!" said Felicity. "But what I don't know is what has happened to Winnie! If she isn't writing these postcards, then who is?!"

Felicity didn't waste any time – she headed straight to the library. It was only last week that she'd seen a film about a fairy who was sent on a secret undercover mission, using someone else's identity. Even though it was a film, it was based on a true story so she knew it could happen in real life. Felicity was desperate to watch the film again, to find out as many tips as she could about how to detect an undercover fairy!

* * *

By the time Felicity received the last postcard, just before Winnie was due home, she was certain that something had happened to her friend.

"I think you'll all agree that this isn't written by Winnie," said Felicity to her friends. "Only a confident fairy would change their plans at the last minute and travel to a different country by themselves."

"Yes," agreed Holly and Polly readily.

"Who is writing the cards then?" asked Daisy.

"Only Miss Meandering knows the answer to that question," said Felicity suspiciously.

"Oh, my goodness!" said Holly, enjoying the drama. "So you think

Miss Meandering must have organized it from the start!"

"Surely not," said Polly sensibly. "Miss Meandering would never do such a thing."

"That's what I thought, at first!" said Felicity. "But you'll never guess what I found when I started to do a bit of research about where Winnie had gone..."

"What? What?" urged Holly, Polly and Daisy.

Felicity took a deep breath and looked over her shoulder to check there were no other fairies listening.

"The island where Winnie is supposed to have gone has... a tree on it."

Holly, Polly and Daisy exchanged confused looks.

"Not just any tree," continued Felicity darkly. "It is *the* tree. The magical rosewood wand tree!"

"The what tree?" asked Holly, completely baffled.

"The magical rosewood wand tree is said to have made the first wand ever held by a fairy hand," said Daisy, who knew about these things. "It has a tiny dent in it where the very first wand known to fairies was carved!"

"Wow!" said Holly. It was the first she'd heard of it.

Suddenly it was obvious to Felicity. Everyone knew that Miss Meandering had a faulty wand. Sometimes, when she waggled it in geography class, the star fell off!

"Miss Meandering must have sent a professional fairy over to the island to carve her a new wand!" gasped Felicity. "And in order to get her there without raising any suspicion, she's taken Winnie's identity."

Polly wasn't convinced. It sounded very unlikely.

Felicity continued, "A professional fairy would have double wings. She would have been able to save the fairies from the sinking ship. She would easily have managed to give that speech in front of the whole school. And travelling alone into unknown countries would be no problem for an advanced fairy."

"Then where is Winnie?" pressed Daisy, who was concerned for her friend's safety.

"That's the bit I don't know!" said Felicity, feeling a little teary.

Polly gave her a big hug. "I know, let's go to Winnie's house and see if we can find any clues!"

* * *

Felicity and her fairy friends quickly flew to Winnie's house. First they checked her bedroom, then they flew round all the other rooms in her house, then they investigated her garden. Then, after a brainwave, they phoned her penfriend, but she hadn't heard from Winnie in weeks.

"There's nothing else left to do," said Felicity resolutely. "We must visit Fairy Godmother and tell her everything!"

* * *

First thing the next morning they arrived at Fairy Godmother's office and knocked on the door. When they were told to enter, Felicity was so distraught she came straight out with her theory, and didn't care how silly it sounded. She just wanted her friend back.

Fairy Godmother put an arm round Felicity and spoke gently to all four fairies. "In many ways, you're right," she said.

"The fairy that sent you these postcards is not the Winnie you knew at school. You will never get your old friend back."

Holly drew in a long shocked breath.

"I knew it!" burst out Felicity. "It was Miss Meandering all along! No fairy ought to be selfish enough to do something like this for her own gain. Especially a teacher! It's outrageous! What in Fairy World has she done with Winnie?"

"Now there's no cause to blame Miss Meandering," cautioned Fairy Godmother. "She's a fine teacher who's only had Winnie's welfare in mind. And don't worry, Winnie is due back to school at any moment. Come along, fairies, I'm sure Winnie will be able to answer all your concerns and put your minds at rest." And, feeling slightly reassured, the fairy friends all fluttered out of her office.

Fairy Godmother took the fairy friends into the assembly hall to sit with the rest of the school. Just as assembly was finishing, she asked everyone to welcome a special guest who was going to give them a short talk on her hopes of becoming an Adventure Fairy when she graduated.

Felicity, Holly, Polly and Daisy couldn't believe their eyes! Out walked a confident Winnie from behind the curtains, smiling and waving at the audience.

She cleared her throat. "I'd always been shy, nervous and quiet before I went away, even with my good friends by my side. But travelling made me realize that there's another part of me that I'd never known before."

The fairy friends stood with their mouths wide open. Winnie looked the same, spoke in the same way, and even fiddled with her wand just as she always had, but she'd become a new person. Felicity held her breath. She couldn't wait for Winnie to continue.

Winnie's eyes twinkled, and she looked straight at Felicity. "When I was travelling alone, I found that it was up to me to be as loud, confident, sensible and studious as my friends had shown me a fairy could be!"

Felicity felt a little silly. She had let her imagination run wild with thoughts of a stolen identity. But, after all, her suspicions about Winnie not being herself were true, in a way.

"So, she is the same Winnie, only different," said Daisy, amused.

"She's the real Winnie," said Polly, "who's reached her true potential through travelling."

"What an incredible journey!" said Holly, already planning which countries she wanted to visit in Fairy World.

"You know what the most incredible thing is?" said Winnie, fluttering over to join her friends with a big hug. "To say thank you to Miss Meandering for choosing me to go on that trip, I've brought her back a present... a wand, cut from the wood of the magical rosewood wand tree!"

"Which just goes to show that you're still you and more! You're the most generous, kind and adventurous fairy friend I know!" said Felicity, giving Winnie an extra big hug.

Believe in yourself

and who knows what could happen

SPARKLE

Marathon Mix-up

Winnie wanted to be an Adventure Fairy when she graduated from the School of Nine Wishes. She wasn't only adventurous in what she did, like climbing mountains, trekking across clouds, and exploring Fairy World. She was also adventurous in how she thought.

Most of Winnie's fairy friends were very careful and safe about how they approached problems or dilemmas. If there was a surprise maths test which meant they had only days to revise, Felicity, Holly, Polly and Daisy would do their best to stay up late and work through their lunch hour to get some revision done.

Winnie was less predictable. Her adventurous heart looked at problems differently. When she was told of a sudden maths test, Winnie approached the problem in an entirely novel way. And in one of her new friends she had found a co-conspirator!

"This surprise maths test is multiple choice, right?" asked Winnie, double-checking.

"Yup," said Felicity, who was leafing through a copy of *Fairy Girl* magazine. "I suppose I should put down my magazine and do some work," she sighed.

"Well," said Winnie, "there's a lot to be said about being relaxed before you do a test like this. A relaxed mind can make better choices. An anxious one might choose the wrong answer in a panic."

"I like your thinking!" said Felicity, picking up her magazine again. "So, reading my magazine and allowing my mind to become relaxed is actually just as good as doing a bit of revision!"

"Better!" said Winnie, smiling and picking up her own magazine. "Although I'm not sure Miss Logic would agree!"

Sometimes having such an adventurous mind helped Winnie in what she wanted to do, but on other occasions it hindered her and even put her at serious risk!

Most fairies have a natural sense of fear. It helps them make judgements about whether to do something or not. In Winnie's brain, her sense of fear was muddled with her sense of excitement… and sometimes this led to disastrous consequences!

"Are you absolutely sure you have the wing strength to do it?" said Polly, looking uncertainly at Winnie's sponsorship form.

"Flying a marathon isn't something just any fairy can do," said Holly. "I've heard horrid stories about fairies' wings literally falling off halfway round!"

Felicity and Daisy winced, looking at Winnie's wings.

"I've flown two half marathons in the last month and I fly to school and back every day," Winnie said, more determined than ever. "If that isn't enough to prepare me, then nothing is! And besides, I have to do it for the sake of the Wingless Fairy Foundation."

Holly nearly spat out a mouthful of milkshake as she tried to contain her giggles. "All the sparkledust you're collecting is going to the Wingless Fairy Foundation?" she choked.

"Yes," said Winnie proudly, taking the form from Polly and showing it to Holly. "How much can I put you down for?"

Holly looked awkward. "Umm, half a bag of sparkledust a mile?"

"Polly's put down a bag a mile," said Felicity, looking over Winnie's shoulder.

"Only because she doesn't think you can finish!" giggled Daisy, nudging Winnie gently.

"OK, OK, I'll put down a bag a mile too!" said Holly reluctantly.

* * *

Winnie hadn't been lying when she said she'd prepared for this race. Over one thousand fairies from all over Fairy World would be competing. Even though Winnie knew she didn't have a hope of winning, she was going to do her best.

"Thirty-six minutes, twelve seconds!" shouted Felicity as Winnie fluttered past her.

Winnie skidded to a bumpy landing and heaved deep heavy breaths before she could speak to her friend.

"Oh, drat!" she gasped, stamping out the last of the energy with her foot. "I really need to fly that stretch in less than thirty minutes if I'm going to reach my personal best on the day of the race."

Felicity hugged her sweaty friend. She'd been coaching Winnie for the last two months and was almost as disappointed as she was.

"It's just the weather!" Felicity ventured. "The wind was against you."

"But the wind might not be behind me on the actual day! I'm never going to make it to the finishing line," said Winnie desperately.

Felicity thought for a moment. "Maybe we could enter the race together, so I can coach you along the way?" she said.

"Would you really do that for me?" asked Winnie, feeling instantly perkier.

"Of course I would," said Felicity. "That's what friends are for."

* * *

"You can't be serious?" said Polly when she heard that Felicity was entering the race too.

"More serious than ever!" said Felicity, proudly linking arms with Winnie.

"But you can barely fly round the netball court without stopping to catch your breath!" said Holly, aghast at what Felicity was contemplating.

"A good friend does all she can to help her friends reach their true potential!" said Felicity. "And if that means joining Winnie in the race to help her on her way, then so be it!"

"You're loopy!" Holly wasn't one to mince her words.

"Felicity," appealed Polly, "I know

friendship means everything to you. But I really don't think you should do this."

Winnie tried to appease Polly's sensible concerns. "It's fine. There will be hundreds of fairies who won't be flying competing in this race. Some of them will be wearing fancy-dress costumes so elaborate that walking will be the only option. Felicity can always walk with them when her wings get too tired."

* * *

On the morning of the marathon, Winnie was more nervous that she'd imagined. She tried hard not to hear all the doubts she had in her mind.

When the fairy friends reached the start, none of them could quite believe the sea of fairies that had gathered. Knowing there would be thousands competing was one thing, but seeing them all together was entirely different.

"We have to stick together, or we'll lose each other in this crowd," urged Winnie, linking arms with Felicity.

"It will soon empty out after the first mile," said Polly, who'd done some research. "If you give it everything you've got for the first leg, you should soon leave the crowds and be flying in a bit of space."

"We'll wait for you at the end!" shouted Holly above the noisy fairy voices.

"Good luck!" called Daisy.

Holly, Polly and Daisy blew kisses, raised hands with crossed fingers and waved as they disappeared into the even bigger crowd of spectators that were lining the start of the race.

Suddenly a hush swept over the mass of fluttering fairy wings.

"On your marks..." came the booming voice over the tannoy. "Get set..." it carried on. "GO!"

And suddenly the sea of fairies erupted. Squeals were heard. Wings waved. And within minutes the whole sky was alive. The atmosphere was electrifying and Felicity soon realized, glancing up, that Winnie wouldn't need help from her. She was flying more quickly than Felicity had ever seen her. Winnie wasn't at the back any more, and she wasn't even in the middle. Winnie was flying with the professional fairies right at the front of the group!

Frantically, Felicity flew as fast as she could, but she wasn't used to so much strenuous exercise and already her wings had started to ache. With every flap her wings felt heavier. She was in such a flutter she could barely see where she was going, and Winnie was nearly out of sight!

Just then and without warning, Felicity was thrown high into the air. She had been so busy trying to trace Winnie that she hadn't been paying attention to what was happening in front of her. She'd ploughed straight into another fairy!

"Oh gosh, oh gosh, oh gosh!" was all Felicity could say as she tumbled through the air, bumping into flying fairies as she went.

Eventually, using all the wing power she could muster, Felicity steadied herself.

"Are you OK?" said a friendly voice. "I'm Tallulah. I saw you tumble from all the way up there." Felicity saw an athletic-looking fairy hovering next to her.

"I'm OK, thank you, but I've lost my  friend," said Felicity, desperately looking around for Winnie.

"Just because you can't find your friend doesn't mean you should give up flying. We can fly together instead if you like. It would really help me, because I've lost my flying partner too," said Tallulah.

And as everyone knew, Felicity could never resist making a new friend.

* * *

Meanwhile, Winnie had almost entirely forgotten about Felicity. In fact, she'd also forgotten about beating her personal best finishing time! The sense of adventure Winnie had in her heart knew no bounds. It acted on spontaneity and excitement. So when Winnie unexpectedly found herself at the front of the race with the professional flying fairies, she could suddenly see the route clearly marked out in front of them... and a whole other exciting adventure.

The race had started at the top of Star Street. The organizers had mapped out a twenty-six mile-long route that took them deep into the countryside and then brought them back into Little Blossoming, over the bridge and finally finished outside the School of Nine Wishes gates.

But the path that Winnie saw in the sky, mapped out in red ribbon, didn't look half as adventurous as the route that they were passing on the ground. Winnie hadn't lived in Little Blossoming long and when they flew over an area that looked like a magical forest she couldn't resist.

"I could just have a peep," she said to herself as she glanced back over her shoulder. "There are hundreds of fairies that are ages behind me and no sign of Felicity. After I've had a little look I can always rejoin the race."

It didn't take Winnie long to dip out of the sky and find herself surrounded by trees and flowers she'd never seen before. Nine Wish Wood was a brand-new adventure just waiting to be discovered.

* * *

Felicity couldn't believe it! It had taken her over four long hours, but with Tallulah by her side she had almost finished the race! Her wings ached, her arms felt weak and her ankles were sore from steering her body in the right direction.

Felicity and Tallulah were flying almost more slowly than they could walk! But as they turned the corner at the bottom of Little Blossoming to cross the bridge, the cheering crowds of shouting fairies did something magical to their energy levels.

From nowhere, Felicity and Tallulah got a burst of energy so powerful that not only did they start to fly faster, they flew with more speed than they had for the whole race.

With only paces to go, Felicity and Tallulah linked hands, and when they finally and jubilantly crossed the finish line, Felicity's fairy friends were there to meet her.

"Well done, Felicity!" screamed the fairies, showering her with hugs and bottles of water.

Felicity wanted to say thank you, but she could hardly breathe, let alone speak!

"Where's Winnie?" asked Holly

when Felicity had caught her breath.

"She was way ahead of me!" said Felicity. "I lost her right at the beginning. She must have finished hours ago."

"But she hasn't even crossed the finishing line yet," said Daisy, confused.

"What a mix-up!" said Polly. "Winnie has obviously got lost. Thank goodness you decided to fly the race, Felicity, or the Wingless Fairy Foundation would never have got all the sparkledust that was pledged on the sponsorship form!"

Suddenly there was a voice from behind them.

"Oh, yes they would, and more!" said Winnie, bursting dramatically over the finish line. "I didn't get lost, or beat my personal best, but I did go on the most fantastic adventure!"

And Winnie pulled from her pockets handfuls of glittering sparkledust she'd gathered from her adventure in Nine Wish Wood.

"It just goes to show that not everything has to go to plan, to be a success," said Felicity, giving her friends a big sweaty hug!

Not everything has
to go to plan

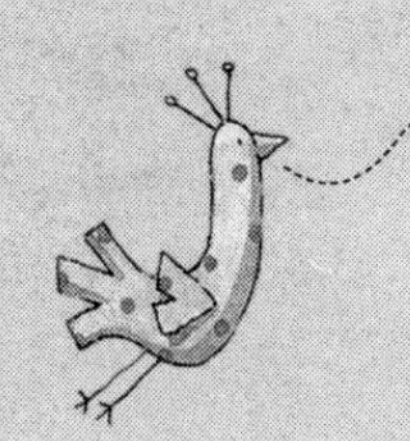

to be a success

Winnie's Wonderland

Felicity Wishes was sitting in Sparkles café with her best friends Holly, Polly and Daisy, talking about their plans for the weekend ahead. Usually the fairy friends spent every minute of every hour together at the weekend – learning new dance routines, listening to Suzi Sparkles' album, and shopping on Star Street. But this weekend they all had errands to run and chores to do.

Polly, Felicity's most organized friend, had an important task to complete for school on Monday. She had to find something the same size and weight as a tooth for a presentation on why she wanted to be a Tooth Fairy when she graduated.

"And I've got an appointment to be fitted for a new crown," said Holly, jiggling her head so that everyone could see how wobbly her old one was. "This one is *so* last season now!"

"I'm flying to the nursery to look at a new delivery of rare and exotic plants," said Daisy, already looking forward to spending the day doing what she loved most. "I'm hoping to find something special for the centre-piece of my front garden."

"Well, I'm going shopping," said Felicity. "My favourite pink purse has broken and I need to find a replacement."

At that moment, Winnie skipped into Sparkles. The previous week, she had been on an extraordinary adventure. She had been flying in a race around her new home of Little Blossoming when she'd seen a magical new part of Nine Wish Wood.

Because she had to finish the race, Winnie had only been able to spend a few moments there discovering some of the secrets that it held. But once the race was over and school was finished for the week, Winnie knew exactly where she was going at the weekend. She couldn't wait to tell her friends about her plans.

"Nine Wish Wood has been by Little Blossoming for ever!" said Felicity. "There are trees in that forest that are older than our school!"

"But we've only ever been to the outskirts of the forest," said Polly. "Fairy Godmother's never been that keen on us going further in, Winnie. At least until we get our double wings."

"The magic that the deep wood contains is too powerful for us novice fairies," explained Daisy.

"I soon realized that when I gave away the sparkledust I'd collected from the star flowers in the wood," said Winnie, who was eager to go back to collect some more. "It lit up with a magical light even when it was nowhere near a wand!"

Felicity, Holly, Polly and Daisy looked uncertainly at their friend. Winnie was an Adventure Fairy at heart and nothing they could do would ever change that. But it didn't stop them from trying to dissuade her.

"The wood certainly seemed magical. But not so magical I'd get into danger," said Winnie, noting her friends' concern. "If I get into trouble, I can always fly out."

Polly wasn't convinced and Winnie could see it.

"Look," said Winnie, having an idea. "Why don't you all come too?"

Holly, Polly and Daisy all had to tell Winnie that they were busy.

"Hmm, I'm supposed to be going shopping," said Felicity, "but I could always go tomorrow." Felicity wanted to be a Friendship Fairy when she left school and she hated letting down a friend in need.

"Great!" said Winnie.

"And we could meet you in the wood for a picnic lunch after we've finished our errands," suggested Polly.

"Yes, let's," said Daisy. "Then we can hear all about your adventure."

* * *

That Saturday, Felicity and Winnie happily winged their way down the high street, over the bridge, across the hills, until finally Nine Wish Wood was within their sight. Winnie had butterflies in her tummy from excitement… and Felicity's tummy rumbled as she thought about their picnic lunch!

Nine Wish Wood was exactly how Winnie remembered it. To any normal fairy it looked just like any other forest. But when you looked more closely you could see that not everything was as it seemed…

The trees had enormous green leaves sheltering secret branches. Each branch supported dozens of sleeping night-birds who clung to their perches with such a grip that even the strongest of winds couldn't disturb their dreams.

The ground of the forest was carpeted with what appeared to be the softest grass Felicity and Winnie had ever walked on. It was only when they knelt down that they realized it wasn't grass at all. Under their feet were thousands of tiny green-petalled flowers that closed up their heads to protect themselves.

"Just listen to the rustle of insects, and look at those magical shimmering butterflies," said Felicity as they wandered deeper into the wood.

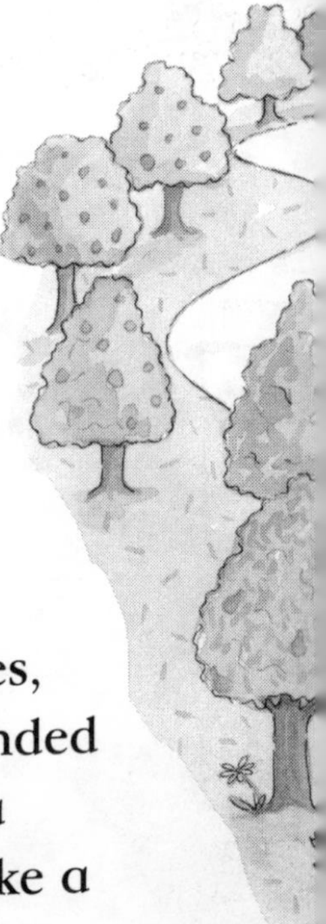

"This is the most enchanted place I've ever been to," said Winnie, completely awestruck.

Then, through the branches, they glimpsed a lake surrounded by fruit trees. It looked like a normal lake, and even felt like a normal lake when Felicity bravely dipped her toes in the cool water. But what the fairies didn't realize at first was that the wonderful aroma of melons and strawberries wasn't coming from the fruit that surrounded them, but from the bubbles that bobbed up from the bottom of the lake to burst on the surface.

"Wow," said Felicity, taking a deep breath in through her nose. "What a delicious smell."

"And how unusual that it should come from the water!" said Winnie, dancing in the foam to intensify the fragrance. But as she twirled she lost her grip on her bag, and watched helplessly as it slid into the lake.

"Oh, goodness," said Felicity, staring deep into the water. "What are we going to do?"

The fairies could just about make out what looked like the handles of Winnie's bag, caught in some plants right at the bottom.

Without a second thought, Winnie dipped into the lake. The weather was warm and she was sure the sunshine would have her clothes dry in no time.

"Erm… are you sure that's a good idea?" asked Felicity nervously. "If Polly was here I'm sure she would tell you to leave your bag there. I bet everything is replaceable."

Felicity walked round the pond. She could just make out Winnie's swimming shape. Suddenly her mobile phone trilled. It was Holly, Polly and Daisy asking for directions.

"You're only seconds away! I'll come and meet you at the edge of the wood," said Felicity. "It'll be easier than giving you directions," she said, knowing that her sense of direction was awful.

Felicity looked into the lake at Winnie. She would only be gone for less than a minute.

* * *

The water was cold and took Winnie's breath away. The strawberry and melon smell was even more wonderful as the bubbles burst right under her nose!

Winnie bobbed up momentarily to take a deep breath, then swam down, deep into the lake. At her old school, Winnie had been school champion for swimming under water!

Inside the lake it was another world. The sounds of the forest were muffled and all Winnie could hear was the beat of her heart. As her eyes adjusted to the blue hue that surrounded everything, she caught a glimpse of her bag. The water was deeper than

she expected and she wasn't sure how much breath she had left!

Dodging fish, bubbles and plants, Winnie dived deeper. The bubbles were making it difficult for her to see properly, and as she finally reached for her bag's handles she realized that she'd have to be quick before her breath ran out.

The gap between the rocks where Winnie's bag had fallen was the same hole that the melon and strawberry bubbles were escaping from. Quickly, with no thought for anything else, Winnie tugged at one of the rocks to release her bag. And as the rock came away in her hand, something amazing happened.

It was as if the whole lake turned inside out. Water began to drain away from the sides until it was the forest that looked as though it was under water and the lake that had become dry land! Winnie couldn't understand it. It took all the courage she had to take a breath through her mouth, just in case what she was seeing was a dream. Breathing normally, Winnie suddenly saw the lake's surroundings in a brand-new way!

"My friends are never going to believe this when I tell them about it!" Winnie said to herself.

"You're right!" said a passing fish.

Winnie nearly fell over with shock!

As if reading her mind, the fish spoke again. "We live in a magical forest, full of magical things. If your friends won't believe you, you should take them something back to show them the magic is real." And with that he floated off.

* * *

"Winnie!" shouted Daisy.

"Winnie!" called out Polly, as she rushed to her friend's side.

"Wake up! Are you OK?" said Felicity desperately.

Slowly, Winnie began to flutter her eyelids and open her eyes. "Where am I? How did I get out of the water?"

"You're in Nine Wish Wood. Whatever happened to you? Are you OK?" asked Felicity.

Winnie sat up and looked at her friends with a very confused look on her face. "You are never going to believe this, but I can breathe under water!" she said slowly.

"I think you've been dreaming!" giggled Daisy.

"I wasn't dreaming, it was real. And I met a fish that could speak," Winnie said, suddenly remembering.

Holly looked at Daisy and Daisy looked at Felicity, who nudged Polly to speak.

"Maybe the dreams that you have here are more magical than the dreams we have at home," reasoned Felicity. "Perhaps that's why Fairy Godmother isn't keen on us playing here until we have our double wings."

Winnie looked around. The lake looked just like any other lake. Perhaps her friends had been right after all: it was understandable that she might be tired and fall into a deep sleep. Last week she had flown a marathon race around Little Blossoming, and today she'd come all the way to the forest. But then out of the corner of her eye she saw her bag, and she knew that it wasn't a dream after all!

"Why don't we start our picnic," suggested Felicity, trying to change the subject. "A double-choc muffin will have you feeling better in no time, Winnie."

"While you've been dreaming," began Daisy, looking at Winnie, "we've all had a horrid morning!"

"I couldn't find a crown that fitted!" moaned Holly, nibbling on a star-shaped cucumber sandwich.

"I couldn't find anything the same size and weight as a tooth for my presentation," sighed Polly.

"And the nursery had run out of exotic plants before I even got there," said Daisy.

"Well then, it's lucky for you all that my dream came true!" said Winnie mysteriously, reaching for her bag.

"This is for you, Holly. I found this at the deepest part of the lake, close to where I retrieved my bag," she said, handing Holly the most spectacular and delicate crown made of coral.

"Oh, how beautiful!" said Holly, removing her wobbly crown and putting the coral one on instead. "It fits perfectly!" she cried, delighted, as she looked into her mirror. "Where did you say you got it?"

"The lake!" said Winnie. "The very same place I got this!"

And she handed Daisy the most beautiful and exotic plant Daisy had ever seen.

"I've never seen anything like this before!" said Daisy, studying the petals. "It looks as if it should be a pond plant, but it's living outside water!"

"This is for you, Polly," said Winnie. She handed her a smooth and perfect white stone, just the same weight and shape as a tooth.

"It's just what I needed! It's almost exactly what I tried so hard to find today!" Polly said in a very surprised voice.

"And," said Winnie, reaching right to the bottom, "the last present from the lake is for you, Felicity." She handed her a perfect pink shell with a tiny pearl button at the top. "You can use it like a purse. Open it, and you'll see!"

Slowly, with disbelieving eyes, Felicity opened up the shell and found a tiny pearl inside. Then she gave Winnie a big hug. The shell would replace her broken purse perfectly!

"So sometimes your dreams can come true – if you really believe in them!" said Felicity, giving Winnie a huge hug.

A true adventure
begins with a risk
of believing in something
you've only ever
dreamed about

The fairies decide to stop being sensible and start having some fun in

Fairy Fun

Sensational Sweets

Felicity Wishes and her friends Holly, Polly, Daisy and Winnie were all feeling a little down in the dumps. It didn't seem as though anything was going right. Each of them had had one sort of catastrophe or another over the last few days. But it was Polly who'd had more than her fair share...

"I've had it!" burst out Polly as she joined her friends at break-time that morning.

"Are you still upset about losing your maths homework on the way to school?" asked Felicity.

Polly shook her head in despair.

"You're not still worried about that stain on the star of your wand?" ventured Holly. "You know, in some fairy countries it's considered lucky when a bird does that!"

Polly looked doubtfully at the end of her wand and grimaced. "Nope," she said. "That's nothing. But on the way to weightlifting class last night my bike got a puncture and by the time I'd mended it I'd missed the entire thing!"

"Oh, no!" said Felicity, hugging Polly. She knew how much weightlifting class meant to her friend. Polly wanted to be a Tooth Fairy when she graduated and it was essential that she was able to lift heavy pillows.

Polly began to sob. All this bad luck really was getting to her.

"You know," she said, imploring her friends, "I always try to do my best. I'm never naughty, I always hand my homework in on time and I keep my house neat and tidy. So why is all this bad luck happening to me?"

Felicity, Winnie, Holly and Daisy looked blankly at their friend. They didn't know what to say.

"Well," said Polly with a new determination in her voice, "if bad luck happens whether you're a conscientious fairy or not then I see little point in trying my best all the time!"

Felicity, Holly, Daisy and Winnie looked at their friend aghast.

"What are you saying?" asked Felicity, fearing the worst.

"I'm saying... I think it's time we stopped being so sensible and started having some fun!"

* * *

The five fairy friends had lost no time getting their new priorities in order. That afternoon, instead of sitting at the front of chemistry class like they usually did, they sat right at the back. They barely listened to a word Miss Sparkle said and instead thought up fantastic fun things to do!

"We could hire super-speed flying bikes for the day," suggested Felicity, "and cycle somewhere we've never been before."

"Or we could check in for a weekend of pampering at the fairy spa," said Daisy.

"I know, let's go to a sweet factory this weekend!" proposed Polly.

Felicity couldn't believe her ears. Polly wanted to be a Tooth Fairy, so she never ever ate sweets!

Miss Sparkle couldn't believe what she was hearing either.

"FAIRIES!" she shouted. "This is no time for gossiping! I'm surprised at you. What's got into you all today? Please mix the two compounds carefully and then come to me to get it marked."

"We can't go to a sweet factory this weekend," said Felicity, whispering over her shoulder. "We've got the school camping trip to the Lakes."

"I'm sure they won't miss us just this once," said Polly, feeling very naughty indeed.

The fairy friends had never seen this rebellious side of Polly and didn't know what to say.

"Sweets or a geography trip," said Polly, waving her wand in the air. "What's more fun?"

The answer was obvious.

* * *

Felicity had never felt the thrill of naughtiness quite so much. They'd all written sick notes to Fairy Godmother, excusing themselves from the school trip.

"Is everyone ready?" said Polly,

hovering excitedly above her fairy friends early on Saturday morning. "Where's Daisy?"

Daisy was notoriously dreamy. One day she wanted to become a Blossom Fairy and she spent most of her time daydreaming about becoming a world-famous gardener.

"She's probably forgotten all about going to the sweet factory and has gone on the geography trip," ventured Felicity.

"We can't go and get her, or Fairy Godmother will see that our excuse about being poorly isn't true!" said Holly.

Polly thought for a moment. "Then we'll have to go without her."

Felicity didn't like to leave Daisy out, but she also didn't want to miss out on such an exciting trip so, reluctantly, she flew off with the others. Felicity had always had a sweet tooth, and this trip was a dream come true.

* * *

But Daisy hadn't forgotten about going to the sweet factory.

Being dreamy meant she thought a lot. And what she thought was that she would spend the whole day worrying about whether they would be found out. She wasn't sure that missing the trip would be as much fun as Polly was promising.

* * *

The sweet factory was more mind-blowing than Felicity had ever imagined. The sugar-coated glass castle stood on a hill so high that it could be seen from miles around. When the sun came up behind the hill it cast brilliantly coloured reflections of the rainbow sweets being made inside.

When they saw its enormous golden

gates, the fairies soon forgot all about the geography trip they were missing and flew inside without a second thought. The magical rainbow exterior was nothing compared to what the fairies found inside. It took their breath away. The castle was divided up into hundreds of glass rooms and leading to these glass rooms were dozens of tiny corridors. Each corridor and room was lit in a different hue of the rainbow.

As Felicity, Holly, Polly and Winnie stood in the grand reception hall they tried hard to find the source of its lilac light. Bafflingly, there wasn't a single sweet in sight.

"Four for the full guided tour," said Polly to the lilac Ticket Fairy behind the counter.

"Are you with a school party?" she asked, looking up at Polly and her single wings. Fully fledged fairies who had graduated from school wore double wings.

Felicity shifted nervously. If the Ticket Fairy found out they were supposed to be on a trip with theSchool of Nine Wishes then Fairy Godmother would be informed instantly.

"Yes, yes, we are. We're doing a special project on the magic of sweets," replied Polly confidently.

Felicity gasped. The Ticket Fairy looked up and gave her a hard frown. Felicity swiftly put her hand over her mouth and pretended that she had actually yawned.

"What sort of school project?" asked the Ticket Fairy suspiciously. It was obvious she didn't believe them.

"On colour!" said Holly quickly, anxious to change the subject. "Where exactly does this lovely lilac colour come from?"

Holly's distraction technique worked

more thoroughly than she'd expected. Half an hour later the fairies were still in the reception hall and none of them had their tickets!

"So you see," said the Ticket Fairy, finally drawing breath, "lilac has always been my favourite colour, and when this job was advertised in *The Daily Flutter* I knew I was made for it. Amazing though, isn't it, that the colour originates from the magic of the sweet itself. This isn't true lilac, of course, it's an overspill from the Blackcurrant Twist booth which is the first room you'll visit on your tour."

"Talking of which..." urged Holly, able to get a word in at last.

"Oh, yes," said the lilac fairy, reaching towards her printer, which whirred out four golden tickets. "If you'd like to walk through to the first room, a fairy will join you shortly for your guided tour."

* * *

The lilac fairy had been right. The beautiful and intense lilac colour the fairies had experienced in the entrance hall was nothing to the rich lilac purple of the Blackcurrant Twist booth. What they didn't expect, though, was to be hit full-on with the sweet smell and taste of blackcurrant itself.

"Oh, wow!" said Felicity, spinning around with an enormous grin on her face. "This is incredible! I feel like I'm inside a blackcurrant!"

Just then a silver panel in the room slid silently back and from behind it came a bubbly fairy, giggling words of welcome.

"So lovely you could come! How super to see you all!" she trilled. "My name is Bella and I will be your guide today."

Felicity, Holly, Polly and Winnie couldn't say a thing. All their mouths were so busy being wide open in shock that no words would come!

Read the rest of

Emma Thomson's Felicity Wishes®

Fairy Fun

to find out what happens

when the fairy friends eat

two-hundred and four sweets each!

If you enjoyed this book, why not try another of these fantastic story collections?

Star Surprise

Designer Drama

Clutter Clean-out

Enchanted Escape

Newspaper Nerves

Whispering Wishes

8
Emma Thomson's
felicity Wishes
friends forever
and other stories
Friends Forever
7
Emma Thomson's
felicity Wishes
Sensational Secrets
and other stories
Sensational Secrets
9
Emma Thomson's
felicity Wishes
Happy Hobbies
and other stories
Happy Hobbies
11
Emma Thomson's
felicity Wishes
Wand Wishes
and other stories
Wand Wishes
10
Emma Thomson's
felicity Wishes
Party Pickle
and other stories
Party Pickle
12
Emma Thomson's
felicity Wishes
Dancing Dreams
and other stories
Dancing Dreams

13
Felicity Wishes
Spooky Sleepover
and other stories
Spooky Sleepover
14
Felicity Wishes
Fashion Fiasco
and other stories
Fashion Fiasco
15
Felicity Wishes
Pink Paradise
and other stories
Pink Paradise
16
Felicity Wishes
Spectacular Skies
and other stories
Spectacular Skies
17
Felicity Wishes
Dreamy Daisy
and other stories
Dreamy Daisy
18
Felicity Wishes
Perfect Polly
and other stories
Perfect Polly

20
19
21
Felicity Wishes
Holly's Hideaway
and other stories
Holly's Hideaway
Felicity Wishes
Winnie's Wonderland
and other stories
Winnie's Wonderland
Felicity Wishes
Fairy Fun
and other stories
Fairy Fun
Look out for these three special editions
Summer Sunshine
Christmas Calamity
Winter Wishes
Felicity Wishes
Christmas Calamity
and other stories
Felicity Wishes
Summer Sunshine
and other stories
Felicity Wishes
with colour illustrations
Winter Wishes
and other stories

Felicity Wishes shows you how to create your own sparkling style, throw a fairy sleepover party and make magical treats in this fabulous mini series. With top tips, magic recipes, fairy products and shimmery secrets.

Sleepover Magic

Cooking Magic

Fashion Magic

Hair Magic

Make-up Magic

Beauty Magic

SEE YOUR FRIENDSHIP
LETTER HERE!
Write in and tell us all
about your best friend, and
you could see your letter
published in one of the
Felicity Wishes books.
Please send in your letter, including
your name and age, with a stamped
self-addressed envelope to:
Felicity Wishes Friendship Competition
Hodder Children's Books, 338 Euston Road, London NW1 3BH
Australian readers should write to...
Hachette Children's Books
Level 17/207 Kent Street, Sydney, NSW 2000, Australia
New Zealand readers should write to...
Hachette Children's Books
PO Box 100-749 North Shore Mail Centre, Auckland, New Zealand
Closing date is 30 April 2007
ALL ENTRIES MUST BE SIGNED BY A PARENT OR GUARDIAN.
TO BE ELIGIBLE ENTRANTS MUST BE UNDER 13 YEARS.
For full terms and conditions visit www.felicitywishes.net/terms

Friends of Felicity

Alice 8 years old

My best friend in the whole world is Phoebe. She is Very Kind and caring. When I feel Sick or dizzy she gets the teacher and looks after me! We always try to pick each other in a lesson at School. I think a good friend Shows every one how to co-operate together

WIN FELICITY WISHES PRIZES!

From January 2006, there will be a Felicity Wishes fiction book publishing each month (in Australia and New Zealand publishing from April 2006) with a different sticker on each cover. Collect all twelve stickers and stick them on the collectors' card which you'll find in *Dancing Dreams* or download from www.felicitywishes.net

Send in your completed card to the relevant address below and you'll be entered into a grand prize draw to receive a Felicity Wishes prize.*

Felicity Wishes Collectors' Competition

Hodder Children's Books, 338 Euston Road, London NW1 3BH

Australian readers should write to...

Hachette Children's Books

Level 17/207 Kent Street, Sydney, NSW 2000, Australia

New Zealand readers should write to...

Hachette Children's Books

PO Box 100-749 North Shore Mail Centre, Auckland, New Zealand

*A draw to pick 50 winners each month will take place from January 2007 - 30th June 2007.

For full terms and conditions visit www.felicitywishes.net/terms

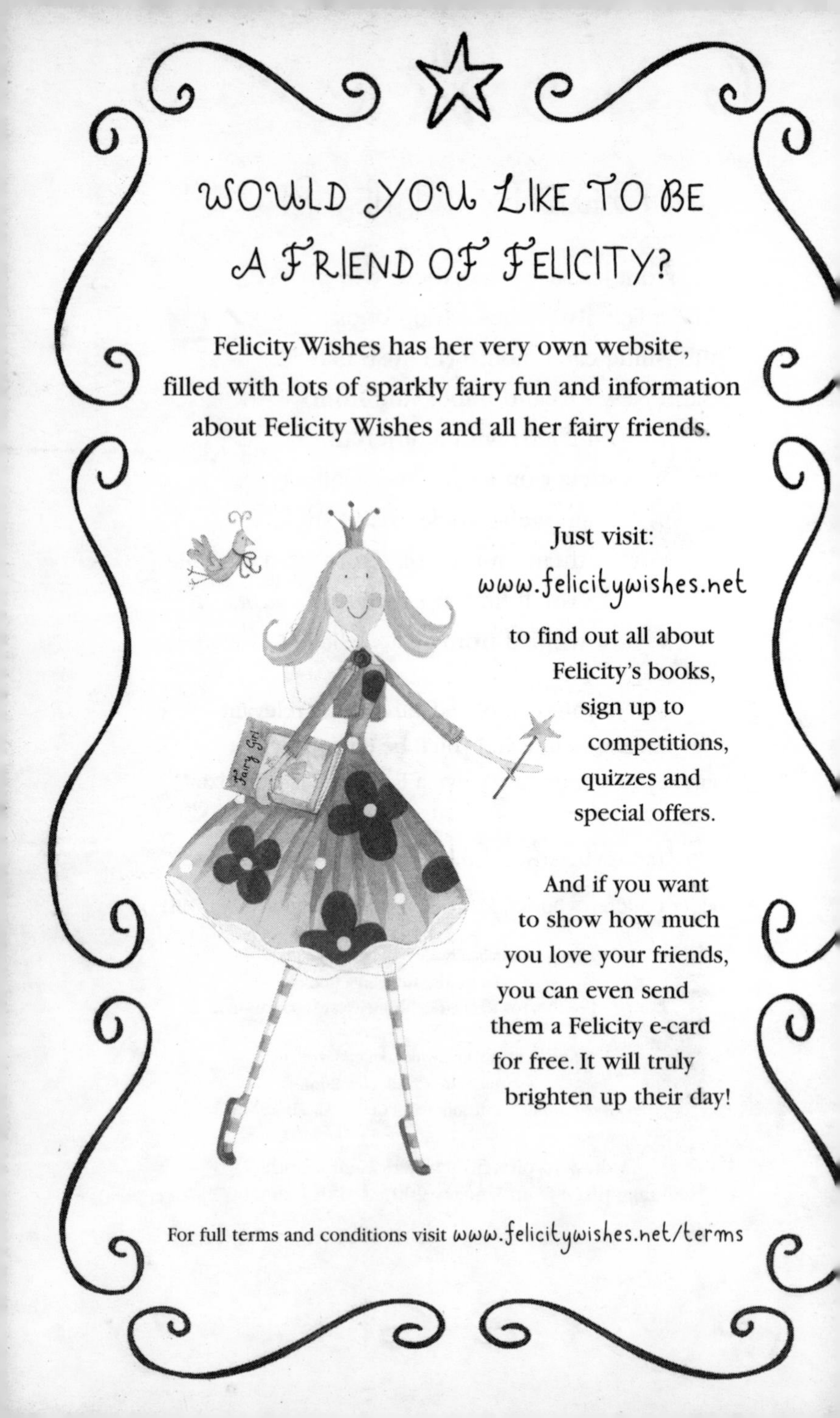
WOULD YOU LIKE TO BE
A FRIEND OF FELICITY?
Felicity Wishes has her very own website, filled with lots of sparkly fairy fun and information about Felicity Wishes and all her fairy friends.
Fairy Girl
Just visit:
www.felicitywishes.net
to find out all about Felicity's books, sign up to competitions, quizzes and special offers.
And if you want to show how much you love your friends, you can even send them a Felicity e-card for free. It will truly brighten up their day!
For full terms and conditions visit www.felicitywishes.net/terms